DEADLY

MISSION

Titles in Teen Reads:

Copy Cat
TOMMY DONBAVAND

Fair Game
ALAN DURANT

Mama Barkfingers
CAVAN SCOTT

Dead Scared
TOMMY DONBAVAND

Jigsaw Lady
TONY LEE

Pest Control
CAVAN SCOTT

Just Bite
TOMMY DONBAVAND

Mister Scratch
TONY LEE

The Hunted
CAVAN SCOTT

Home
TOMMY DONBAVAND

Stalker
TONY LEE

The Changeling
CAVAN SCOTT

Kidnap
TOMMY DONBAVAND

Dawn of the Daves
TIM COLLINS

Nightmare
ANN EVANS

Ward 13
TOMMY DONBAVAND

Joke Shop
TIM COLLINS

Sitting Target
JOHN TOWNSEND

Deadly Mission
MARK WRIGHT

The Locals
TIM COLLINS

Snow White, Black Heart
JACQUELINE RAYNER

Ghost Bell
MARK WRIGHT

Troll
TIM COLLINS

The Wishing Doll
BEVERLY SANFORD

The Corridor
MARK WRIGHT

Insectoids
ROGER HURN

Underworld
SIMON CHESHIRE

Death Road
JON MAYHEW

Billy Button
CAVAN SCOTT

World Without Words
JONNY ZUCKER

Badger Publishing Limited, Oldmedow Road, Hardwick Industrial Estate, King's Lynn PE30 4JJ
Telephone: 01438 791037

www.badgerlearning.co.uk

DEADLY MISSION

MARK WRIGHT

Deadly Mission ISBN 978-1-78147-803-5

Text © Mark Wright 2014
Complete work © Badger Publishing Limited 2014

Publisher: Susan Ross
Senior Editor: Danny Pearson
Publishing Assistant: Claire Morgan
Copyeditor: Cheryl Lanyon
Designer: Bigtop Design Ltd
Printed by Bell and Bain Ltd, Glasgow

2 4 6 8 10 9 7 5 3

CHAPTER 1

The man ran.

He sprinted along the street, clutching a hand to his shoulder. When he pulled it away, it was wet with blood. He quickly unzipped his black combat jacket. A red stain was spreading across the white T-shirt.

A car engine growled at the end of the quiet street. Had they found him? He looked left and right, then ducked between two parked cars, ignoring the throbbing pain in his shoulder as he ran across the road.

Was the car following? He couldn't tell. Couldn't look. Had to get to…

The man stopped to look at the sign on the wall next to a gate. **Blackthorne High School**. He pushed open the metal gate and sprinted across the empty playground.

*

"So, if we think about the themes of the book and what the author is saying," said Miss Maslen at the front of class, "that should help when you come to write the book report."

Hildy rested her head on her hand, concentrating on Miss Maslen's words. English was her favourite subject, but it was a sunny afternoon and the corridors and classrooms of Blackthorne High were hot and sleepy. Two desks across sat her friend Ryan. She caught his eye and he grinned back. Luca was next to Ryan. He leaned in, running a hand through his deliberately messy black hair and rolled his eyes.

"I take it from your attentive silence that you've all got that?"

As one, the class laughed. "Yes, miss!"

*

A car screeched to a halt. Three men scrambled out, looking frantically up and down the street.

"He can't have got far!" growled one.
"Keep looking."

The others grunted and fanned out along the pavement. All three were heavily built, wearing identical black leather jackets, dark blue jeans and black shades.

"It's a school," one called to the leader, looking up at the sign that said Blackthorne High School.

There was a flash of movement, causing the man to look across the playground. Through his dark shades he saw a door open into the main school building. "There!" he snarled. "He's in the school!"

The three men ran into the school, a moving wall of leather and denim.

*

"When you finish the report, go through it," advised Miss Maslen. Hildy always enjoyed writing book reports, but as the afternoon went on she was equally looking forward to being out in the sunshine with her friends.

"See if you can find ways to make it more entertaining for the reader." Miss Maslen smiled. "Otherwise known as me."

*

He opened the door and peered into the room. The pain in his shoulder was getting worse. The cloakroom was quiet and he slipped in, dust swirling in a shaft of sunlight. Bags and coats lined the walls.

They were here. He knew they'd seen him and wouldn't be far behind. Stupid, leading them inside the school, but he'd had no choice. No point worrying now. He had to act.

A bang somewhere in the distance. Movement. He glanced through the window. He could see another windowed corridor opposite the cloakroom, separated from it by a grass lawn. Three leather-jacketed men stalked quickly along the corridor as if they owned the place.

The man looked around. This was what he was trained for, but his mission was about to go horribly wrong. He didn't dare think about what that meant, only…

There was one way out of this. Risky, but he'd run out of options.

As the men neared the end of the corridor, he opened his jacket. His T-shirt was soaked with blood now and he felt dizzy. He gritted his teeth and pulled out a thin, grey plastic case. He undid the straps on the nearest bag and slipped it inside.

Boot steps thudded on the corridor outside. They were here. He staggered across to the other door, head pounding, getting weaker.

As he pushed the door open he was dimly aware of the door behind him smashing open and three heavily-built figures thundering after him.

He ran. There was always a lot of running in his job.

And as he ran, he only had one thought: *have I done the right thing?*

*

Twenty minutes later, students streamed out of Blackthorne High. Another day ended. Laughter. Excited shouts.

With Ryan and Luca on either side, Hildy laughed and joked with them as they started their walk home. She hefted her bag onto her shoulder and didn't notice the three men standing by a silver car.

CHAPTER 2

"Got anything to eat?" Ryan asked, opening the fridge door in Hildy's kitchen.

Hildy put her bag on the table. "Think there's some cold chicken. Or make some toast. There's Marmite."

Luca made a gagging sound. "That stuff's gross," he laughed, getting his books out. They usually went to one of their houses after school. It was a deal they had with their parents – they got to hang out as long as they did homework.

Ryan plonked a plate of cold chicken on the table. "You're a pig," joked Hildy.

"Yeah, but a happy pig." He took a bite. "What are we doing?"

"Book report for Miss Maslen," said Luca.

Hildy opened her own bag. "If I get this and my project work done before the weekend, I can go orienteering with Dad on Saturday."

"Cool," said Ryan, without much enthusiasm.

Hildy emptied her books onto the table. "He reckons my map reading's really coming on. If we – "

A small package tumbled out onto the table amongst her books. "What's wrong?" asked Luca.

"This isn't mine," Hildy replied. She carefully picked it up. It was thin and rectangular, made from tough, grey plastic.

"What is it?" asked Luca.

Hildy held up the odd-looking package to examine it closer. "No idea."

The three friends stared at the object. Hildy broke the silence. "I'm opening it."

Ryan shot up from his chair. "What if it's a bomb?"

"It isn't a bomb, you doughnut," sighed Luca.

Hildy felt along the edge of the smooth plastic box. "There's a catch at the end."

Ryan's face creased in alarm as he backed against the wall. Luca nodded at Hildy. There was a tense second as she fumbled with the catch. Ryan breathed in.

Click.

The box opened.

Ryan breathed out.

Hildy fully opened the thin edge of plastic. A small, square object clattered onto the table, followed by a square of stiff paper.

"I don't get it," said Ryan.

Luca leaned forwards and carefully picked up the object. "Don't think any of us do." As he examined it, Hildy looked at the paper. "What do you reckon?" he asked. It looked to be a component to slot into a computer, each edge lined with a minute row of jagged metal teeth.

Ryan shrugged. "Integrated circuit? Haven't done much on this stuff in computer science." Of all his school subjects, anything with a keyboard and screen usually excited Ryan. "This looks wrong, though." He pointed to the gem-like centre of the circuit. It almost glowed with green light, thin lines of silver snaking out from it to the edge of the board. "Could ask Mr Scott tomorrow."

"Could be too late," said Hildy, her freckled nose wrinkling as she studied the paper. She held it up for the boys, pointing to a line of numbers:

SD 93640 34092

"That's a map grid reference," explained Hildy. "Been doing it with Dad on our orienteering days at the nature reserve."

Ryan didn't look impressed. "So?"

"That isn't what worries me."

Luca grabbed the paper from her, reading the word printed in large, red letters beneath the map reference:

URGENT!

Goosebumps prickled Hildy's arms. "Somebody wants this. Badly."

CHAPTER 3

The three friends didn't have much time to talk about their discovery. Hildy's mum arrived home and started making tea – the signal for Luca and Ry to head home. She looked at the three in concern and suspicion, commenting that they all looked like they'd seen a ghost.

But they still had lots of questions:

1 What was the circuit for?

2 Where was the map reference?

3 Who wanted it; and why was it urgent?

4 Who had left the package in Hildy's bag? (This last one had left Hildy with a sick feeling.)

Ryan was the sensible one for a change – he suggested they kept hold of the package and handed it to Mrs Albiston, the headteacher, in the morning. Job done. They split up for the evening, agreeing this was probably the best plan.

But Hildy couldn't let go of the feeling that something was very wrong. The circuit had been left there on purpose and she was meant to find it.

That night she helped her mum with some chores and made plans with her dad for their orienteering trip to the nature reserve on Saturday. She tried to be chatty and upbeat, but the word URGENT! kept flashing in front of her eyes.

She sat at the desk in her room for what seemed like hours, turning the circuit over in her hand. The green gem reflected the light of her lamp, casting emerald patterns around her room. Even in bed, Hildy couldn't leave it alone, sitting up in bed.

Tomorrow, it wouldn't be her – or her friends'
– problem. They'd hand it over to their
headteacher and she could take it to the police.

Hildy slid the paper and circuit back into the
casing. She clicked off the bedside lamp and
snuggled under the duvet.

*

"What – ?"

Hildy was wide awake. A car door slammed out
on the street. What time was it? It was still dark;
she could have been asleep for minutes; or hours.
She had a sudden panicked thought, but it was
OK. The plastic case was still on her bedside
table.

She tiptoed over to the window and peered
through a crack in the curtain. Streetlamps cast
their orange glow on the ranks of parked cars
that lined either side of the street. Quiet. Maybe
she'd imagined –

A figure detached itself from a shadow and walked across the street. Leather jacket. Jeans. Shades? Who wore shades at night? Hildy saw two identically clothed figures further up her road. Moving slowly, calmly. Searching.

Hildy hardly dared breathe as the first man stopped outside her house; he looked up, shaded eyes resting on each window in turn. She gasped, stepping back as he seemed to look directly at her.

The man placed a hand on the gate. In seconds he'd be in the front garden. Then what? In the house? She should call for her mum and dad, phone the police...

Just as he was about to open the gate, the man stopped. A beam of white light shone at the end of the road, a distant engine. He stepped back, looking. The lights vanished, the car moved off.

'Shades' (as Hildy named him to herself) looked back at the house, then directly at Hildy. She didn't flinch, but stared straight back. He raised a hand, fingers arranged in a child's approximation of a gun. He grinned and brought his thumb down.

His meaning was clear.

BANG!

He turned and walked slowly to a sleek, silver car parked up the street. All three men slid into the car. She expected it to drive off, but it remained still. Just another parked car on a suburban street.

Hildy almost collapsed to the floor, pulling her knees up and placing her back to the wall. It felt cool and safe.

It didn't take a genius to work out what the men were after. She looked at the package resting on her bedside cabinet.

CHAPTER 4

Hildy was up and dressed before it was light. She crept downstairs wearing running bottoms, trainers and a waterproof hoodie, just as night was turning into silvery dawn.

She placed the package containing the circuit into a rucksack. She paused in the kitchen and saw her dad's tablet computer. With a look upstairs she whispered, "Sorry, Dad," and slipped it in with the package.

Next stop: water from the fridge, bags of crisps and some apples.

She stayed close to the wall and peered through the lounge window. The silver car was still there. Waiting.

Hildy's heart beat faster but, without a second's hesitation, she went to the back door, unlocked and opened it. She paused to listen. No movement from upstairs. Then she was through and out into the garden.

All the houses on Hildy's street had gardens backing onto the houses in the next street, their gardens separated by tall fences. The air was starting to fill with a dawn chorus as Hildy moved silently across the lawn and up to the fence.

She leaped onto the plastic composter, feeling as if somebody else was in control of her movements. She threw the rucksack over, gripped the top of the fence and pulled herself over, too. It was a bit more of a drop than she'd expected and she landed heavily.

But she was over.

Grabbing the dropped rucksack, she padded quickly towards the house. Her family was good friends with Mr Cowan, and if she'd timed this right…

She reached the door as it opened, a golden Labrador leaping out and bolting for the bottom of the garden.

"Morning Mr C," said Hildy to the confused man in the dressing gown clutching a coffee cup.

 "Hildy?" he mumbled.

"Sorry! Figured you'd be up to let Lucy out."

"What's going on?" Mr Cowan was now wide awake.

"Training for, uh, sports' day," she said, gesturing into the house. "Can I – ?"

Mr Cowan stepped aside. "Be my guest."

"Thanks!" Hildy ran into the house, leaving Mr Cowan shaking his head.

"Young 'uns," he said, wearily.

She ran to the front of the house and let herself out. The street was almost identical to hers – lines of houses and parked cars. She turned left out of the gate, running steadily to the end of the street.

Now the tricky bit…

She kneeled and peered round the wall into her own street. The silver car was closer than expected, the windows so dark she couldn't tell if the men were inside or not.

She'd have to risk it.

One. Two. Three.

Keeping low, Hildy darted across. She thought about her mum and dad. What would they think when they realised she wasn't there? But she had to keep them out of danger.

She reached the other side of the road and kept running. There didn't seem to be any sign of pursuit.

She'd done it!

*

"Wake up!"

Ryan groaned under his duvet, opening his eyes. Hildy and Luca looked down at him. "Hey, this is my bedroom!"

"Well done," sighed Luca.

"Get up, we've got problems," said Hildy.

"You're not kidding," grumbled Ryan, wide awake. "Why are you two wearing sports' gear? It's a school day."

"We're not going to school," said Hildy. "Now, get up!"

Ten minutes later, Ryan was dressed and up to speed with Hildy's adventures.

"Why don't we take it to the police?" asked Ryan. Hildy pulled out her dad's tablet.

"Hildy reckons it'll take too much time and we'll be too late," said Luca.

Ryan frowned. "For what?"

"For whoever needs the circuit." Hildy tapped a few times and the tablet's map app filled the screen. She pointed at a flashing blue dot. "This is your house, Ry. And this…" she tapped again, "is the map reference on the paper."

"It's in the middle of nowhere," moaned Ryan.

Hildy turned to her friends. "It's about twelve miles, up on the moor. I've been up there with Dad."

"You want to go there?" Luca sounded unsure.

"Remember what it said on the paper?" Hildy was serious. "Urgent."

"But," started Ryan, "what about school? Let's just tell Mrs Albiston."

"No!" Hildy's freckled face was set in determination. "I just know we need to do this, and stop those big guys from getting the circuit."

"What do you think, Ry?" asked Luca.

Ryan threw his hands up in defeat. "Girls!"

CHAPTER 5

The bus pulled away with a roar, leaving Hildy, Ryan and Luca looking out across bleak moorland. Dark clouds drifted overhead and a cold breeze blew across the green and brown landscape. If it weren't for the bus stop you wouldn't know that civilisation was just a few miles away.

They'd managed to catch the bus in town without incident, although three out-of-school teenagers, standing at a bus stop in hiking gear, had received odd looks from commuters.

Ryan shivered and zipped his waterproof. "Which way?"

Hildy pulled out her dad's tablet. "No signal." Luca and Ryan checked their phones, with the same result.

A look of panic spread across Luca's face. "What now? If we can't check our location…"

Hildy unzipped her rucksack. "Ordnance Survey map," she explained, pulling out a folded document. "Thought we might have this problem."

Together they weighted the corners down. The tip of Hildy's tongue stuck out as she concentrated. "We're here," she pointed to the map, then stabbed a finger on it, right at the heart of the moor. "We want to be here."

"Don't say it, Ry," said Luca when Ryan opened his mouth to speak. "It's a long way, we know."

Hildy pulled out a plastic compass. She placed it flat on the map, rotating the dial to identify north in relation to their location. She rotated the dial again, drawing a line in pencil from one point to another.

"Got it!" she said, pointing across the deserted landscape. "That way." Luca and Ryan looked impressed. "And you two think orienteering's daft."

*

The three friends walked in silence, the grass swishing beneath their feet. They were lost in their own thoughts. Had they been missed? How much trouble would they be in at school? When was lunch? Were they doing the right thing?

Hildy looked over at the boys walking beside her. She knew she was asking a lot of them, but she was glad they were there. Good mates, both of them.

The only sound on the moor was the breeze. They were utterly alone.

Hildy hoped it stayed that way.

*

They made good progress, scrambling up slopes, scrabbling down the other side. They crossed a stream, splashing through freezing cold water, all the while getting closer to their goal.

Whatever that might be...

After an hour, Hildy thought they could risk a stop – at least to shut Ryan up; he'd complained about being hungry since they'd set off. They sat on clumps of grass in the shadow of a steep incline, drinking water and munching on crisps and apples.

Luca was quiet, but Ryan babbled on, nervously. "You and your dad do this sort of thing for fun?"

"Yeah," she shrugged. "I like it. Whole family goes walking a lot."

Ryan screwed up his empty crisp packet. "Computers and books, that's my thing."

Hildy smiled. "I know. We've been mates for five years."

"Oh yeah," laughed Ryan. "What about you, Luca? How are Liverpool – "

A few feet away, some loose rocks tumbled down an incline. They jumped to their feet, listening in silence. Nobody moved, all three waiting for a hand on their shoulder – or worse. But nothing happened.

Luca's face was serious. "This is crazy," he whispered. "We're kids. We could get caught at any time. Who knows what they'd do to us?"

Hildy zipped her rucksack, checking the package was safe. "Just 'cos we're kids, doesn't mean we can't help."

"I'm scared," said Luca, shoulders sagging.

Hildy placed a hand on his shoulder. "Me too." She smiled and he smiled back. "That's why we've got to keep going, prove that kids aren't a waste of space."

CHAPTER 6

"We're lost, aren't we?"

"We're not lost, Ry, I'm taking another bearing." Hildy was hunched over the map, turning the dial on her compass, making their route as accurate as possible.

Luca looked out across the never-ending moor. "How far do you reckon we've come?"

"Nearly five miles." Hildy stood, shouldering the rucksack. "Another three to go."

Ryan opened his mouth to complain, then thought better of it when he saw the glaring looks from Hildy and Luca. "OK, let's go."

"What if there's nothing there?" asked Luca. "Well?"

Hildy ignored the question.

They trudged on, moorland rising ahead of them, but now the ground evened out and began to slope down. Hills rose and fell towards the horizon, grey clouds darkening further.

Even Ryan had to admit it was a cool view, the fact that they were going downhill lifting his spirits.

Dirt banks rose on either side of them, the grass giving way to a rough dirt track. They were now walking through a wide gulley, feet crunching on dry ground. Thunder rumbled in the distance. Ryan looked around nervously.

"Don't be a baby," said Luca.

"It's not that," he replied. "Can cope with a bit of thunder. Get the feeling we're being watched."

"Don't be daft," said Hildy. "We're the only ones here."

As if to prove her wrong, a motorbike jumped from the top of the banking, engine shrieking. The helmeted rider brought it down in a spray of dirt.

The three friends looked around frantically. The bike span in an arc before coming to a halt, engine purring, the rider facing the terrified teenagers.

Hildy watched in horror as the mirrored helmet visor was lifted, revealing a pair of shades. She knew she was facing the same man who had looked up at her window the night before.

Shades.

"It's them," she breathed.

"What do we do?" demanded Ryan, panicking. Shades grinned, pulled the helmet visor down and gunned the engine. The bike shot forwards.

"Run!" shouted Hildy. As one, they ran in the opposite direction, but the biker was on them in a second, raising a booted foot. It struck Ryan on the leg, sending him falling with a cry.

"Ry!"

"I'm all right," he said, clambering to his feet. A short distance away the bike stopped, spinning back to face them.

"He's coming round," said Luca. "We've got to get out of this gulley!"

"Make for the ridge!" shouted Hildy. They sprinted, trainers thudding. A spray of fine rain began to fall. The bike engine roared. Hildy was aware of a dim shape rapidly approaching from behind. Just as it seemed they would be crushed under the wheel, Hildy, Luca and Ryan scattered in different directions. The bike shot past, engine screaming as Shades tried to brake, but it was too late. It skidded sideways and slammed into the banking at one side of the gulley.

"Yes!" gasped Hildy.

"Come on!" urged Luca, pushing Ryan forwards. "He'll soon be up."

They didn't wait to find out. They ran. Ryan was red faced but he kept going, all three looking forwards to where the track rose up from the gulley.

"If we can… make it up… there," breathed Hildy. Then they heard it. A motorbike engine. Then another. And another.

The friends turned. The first bike had been joined by two more, speeding towards them from the gulley in a triangle formation. The riders' faceless helmets made them look like terrifying aliens.

Hildy was fit but her lungs screamed. One foot in front of the other. Thud. Thud. Thud. It didn't take a genius to realise the bikers would soon catch them.

But she had to keep going. She felt the rucksack bouncing on her back. For whoever needed the circuit, she had to keep going.

"Hildy, I can't – " Ryan could barely breathe.

"Don't look back!" shouted Luca.

They were almost out of the gulley. The engines buzzed like insects, closer and closer.

Hildy reached the top first, sprinting out onto the rise, hope surging through her. Then she stopped sharply as the path fell away. Luca and Ryan cannoned into her, forcing Hildy to windmill her arms back to stop herself falling.

"What – ?" gasped Luca. Ryan just sucked in deep lungfuls of air.

The path stopped, the ground falling away into a deep valley. Hills stretched out into the distance, clouds blackening on the horizon. Directly beneath them, far down in the valley, nestled an enormous reservoir of dark water.

The three motorbikes roared up behind them. They had nowhere else to go. Trapped!

The lead biker killed his engine and pulled off his mirrored helmet, looking at the three terrified friends through dark shades.

"End of the line, kids."

CHAPTER 7

"Get off them!" screamed Hildy, as Luca and Ryan were grabbed by two of the bikers. Luca and Ryan struggled as they were dragged away from the edge.

"This can be as easy, or as hard as you like," said Shades, holding out a hand. "Give me the circuit and this will all be over."

"No," said Hildy defiantly.

"You wouldn't want your friends to get hurt."

Hildy's eyes darted from side to side. Shades faced her, with Luca and Ryan at either side, struggling in the grip of the bikers, gloved hands clamped over their mouths. Behind her, nothing but empty space. She took a deep breath.

"This what you want?" she asked, pulling the grey plastic container from her rucksack.

"Hand it over," hissed Shades.

"Why?" She slid the container back into the rucksack, out of sight.

The leader gestured to his men. A second later, guns were held to Luca and Ryan's heads. "Because I'll kill your friends if you don't."

Hildy's heart raced and she tried to stop her hand shaking. Shades's voice softened as he took a step forwards. "Come on, we're the good guys. We need that circuit."

"Good guys don't threaten kids with guns!"

"You're messing with things that don't concern you, little girl." Shades took another pace. Hildy stepped back towards the edge.

She glanced quickly back, then at Luca and Ryan. The guns were still rammed into their temples. Luca's eyes were wide with fear, but Ryan moved his head from side to side.

No.

Hildy held the rucksack up high. "You want it? Come and get it!"

Shades lunged forwards. Luca and Ryan struggled. Hildy hurled the rucksack with all her strength. It arced upwards, turning over and over as it soared over the valley. The world fell silent as the rucksack dropped. It grew smaller and smaller, before hitting the surface of the reservoir far below.

"You stupid girl," snarled Shades, turning from the edge to face Hildy.

But she had gone.

*

As soon as the rucksack hit the water, Hildy sprinted along the ridge of the hillside. She was aware of Luca slamming his foot down hard on his captor's boot, causing him to fall back with a cry, but then they were lost from sight.

She felt in her pocket. Yes! Still there. The circuit, safely transferred from its box before the rucksack was hurled to a watery grave. Her trainers slipped on the grass, threatening to send her flying over the edge, but she kept her balance and carried on.

Hildy didn't need to look back to know that Shades wasn't far behind. She saw the dark ring of the reservoir out of the corner of her eye, dominating the landscape below. That had to be where the map reference had brought them to.

"C'mere!" Shades shouted. She ran on, and Hildy knew he would soon be on her. And then? Who knew what these desperate men would do.

A hand swiped out, brushing the hood of her jacket. It slipped off, but next time Hildy wouldn't be so lucky. She sucked in a painful breath, hoping that Ryan and Luca were OK. Then, as Shades lunged towards her, she closed her eyes and jumped.

Hildy dropped through space, her stomach turning somersaults. It felt as though minutes passed before she hit the ground as it sloped away in a sharp arc from the sheer bank. Air was forced from her lungs and she tumbled over and over. Her arm struck a rock and she cried out. Just as it seemed she would never stop falling, she began to slow, coming to a halt in a tangled heap.

Every muscle in her body ached, her arm throbbed painfully, and she just wanted to curl up in a ball. But even though it hurt, even though she was exhausted, she dragged herself to her feet and looked around.

The hillside rose up behind her and a short distance away a grass bank sloped up towards the edge of the reservoir. Cut into the slope was a long set of stone steps going up towards a metal door that must lead down to beneath the reservoir. She didn't know what she'd find there, but knew instinctively that that's where she needed to go.

Hildy turned to see Shades looking down from the top of the hill, pointing. There was no sign of the others. Holding her painful arm against her body, Hildy ran.

Hildy pounded up the stone steps, strength draining from her legs, but she refused to give up. Each step sent pain stabbing through her, but that pain gave her the strength to continue. The steps levelled out and she sprinted the rest of the way to the door.

The locking mechanism was a metal lever, which she pulled on. With a shriek of straining metal, it began to move. She heaved the heavy, reinforced door open, expecting to feel the iron grip of her pursuer on her jacket at any second.

She was through, and ran into the darkness beyond.

*

Hildy found herself on a steep, dimly-lit metal staircase that disappeared in the darkness ahead. A light fizzed on and off further down, and water dripped from walls slick with moisture.

"Going down," sighed Hildy and began to descend, regretting that she hadn't packed a torch. Her footsteps echoed on the metal walkway, which went deeper and deeper beneath the reservoir.

A pool of dirty, yellow light illuminated the bottom of the staircase. Hildy stepped cautiously from the last step, glancing back. Still no sign of pursuit. Ahead she could see a door, its frame illuminated by a thin rectangle of bright, white light.

This was it. This was why she had risked her life, the life of her friends. On their walks and orienteering trips, her dad had always told her to trust her instincts. That's all she'd done today.

She stood before the door and hoped it was enough.

Light and noise exploded into the corridor when she pushed the door open, destroying the silence. Hildy saw a large, high-ceilinged room ahead, blinding white light shining somewhere within, a high-pitched whine like a crying dog filling the air. She shielded her eyes with her hand and stepped forwards.

Three walls of the room were lined with banks of equipment, lights blinking on and off across their surfaces. The fourth wall was taken up with a window of thick glass, and in front of this sat a man in a white lab coat, his fingers dancing over a computer keyboard. Behind the window, white light blasted, casting beams across the walls.

Whatever Hildy had been expecting, it wasn't this. She swallowed, her mouth dry. "Hello," she said. Then louder, "Hello!"

The man whipped round, his thin, angular face desperate, black smudges ringing tired eyes. "Who the hell are you?" he demanded. "This is a quarantined area!" His fingers never left the keyboard, constantly tapping. Hildy ran to him.

"What is this place?" asked Hildy, shouting to be heard.

"That's classified! Everybody was supposed to be evacuated when the reactor went into overload."

"You're still here," Hildy pointed out.

"Somebody had to stay to keep the reactor under control until help came." Beyond the window, sparks of white lightning snaked over the walls. "Unless you have a death wish, get out of here quickly!"

It took Hildy a moment to realise that she was that help. She pulled the circuit from her pocket. "This what you're looking for?"

The man almost did a double-take. "Where did you get that?"

"It's a long story!"

Hildy held the circuit out.

"I wouldn't, if I were you." The click of a gun cocking stopped Hildy dead. Shades stood in the doorway, his gun covering them. "Hand it over!"

"Are you insane?" the scientist demanded. "If that circuit isn't placed in the system, this whole facility is going up, taking us with it!"

"I've come a long way for that, it's worth a lot of money to my employers." He gestured with the gun. "Hand it over!"

Hildy looked across the control board, the noise in the room deafening now. A slot just above the keyboard looked the perfect size for the circuit.

Trust your instincts…

Everything happened at once. Shades raised the gun, finger squeezing the trigger. The scientist threw himself at the man, trying to pull the gun from his grip. Hildy's hand moved the circuit towards the slot. The scientist was thrown back onto the floor.

"No!" Hildy looked straight at Shades as he brought the gun round to point straight at her. She closed her eyes and rammed the circuit home with a click. A shot rang out as power flowed through the gem at the centre of the circuit, a spark of green lightning blasting out, striking Shades square in the chest. He slammed against the wall, his gun clattering to the floor. His body jerked, then he was still.

In the silence that followed, the scientist pulled himself to his feet and ran to check his control board. He breathed out in relief. "You did it. The reactor's under control."

Hildy looked at the prone form of the man who had pursued her across the moors, noticing that he was still breathing. She started to laugh.

"What's so funny?" asked the scientist.

Hildy pointed. "He's still wearing his shades."

CHAPTER 8

Hildy, Luca and Ryan sat in the back of an ambulance, red blankets draped around their shoulders. They sipped from mugs of hot, sweet tea.

The friends had swapped stories about their experiences. Ryan and Luca had managed to evade their captors, throwing their guns over the edge. They'd tried to come after Hildy, but the bikers had blocked their way, then they just rode off on their bikes when Shades didn't return.

"You're making it up!" exclaimed Ryan when Hildy told her own story, but then he grinned.

"What happens now?" asked Luca. The three friends looked at each other, shrugging. Just then a man walked up to the back of the ambulance.

"Hi kids, how's it going? I'm Agent Brennan of the…" he stopped. "Well, you don't need to know which department I'm with."

"Are you like James Bond?" asked Ryan.

Agent Brennan laughed. "Not exactly. You guys have been very brave and have averted what could have been a disaster. This station is involved in some pretty heavy research into…" he stopped again.

"Let me guess," smiled Hildy. "Classified?"

"You got it," laughed Brennan, wincing and holding a hand to his shoulder.

"What did you do?"

"I had a run-in with your friends on the bikes. I was the one bringing the circuit to the station –

it's pretty sensitive stuff up here, and sometimes the government needs to do things off the beaten track. I put the circuit in your bag in the school. It was the only thing I could think of."

Hildy shrugged. "It's OK, I needed the exercise. Why did those guys want it?"

"There are enemy powers that would pay a lot for anything connected to this research. I'm sorry you had to get involved."

"Buy me a pizza and we'll call it quits," said Ryan, then gasped, "Ow!" when Luca punched him on the arm.

"There'll be a full debrief of course," explained Brennan, "and you'll have to sign the Official Secrets Act."

"Cool," said Luca.

"What about the other bikers?" asked Hildy. "Aren't they dangerous?"

Brennan grinned. "Don't worry. That's all taken care of."

*

Wind whipped across the moor, a sudden rumble of thunder mixing in with the growl of motorbike engines. Two bikes bounced across a rough dirt track, coming to a halt in a spray of mud.

The leather-jacketed men pulled their helmets off. Still wearing black shades, they looked around urgently.

"Think we did it," grunted one. "Nobody following."

The other nodded, relieved, a look that quickly turned to alarm as multiple rifles were loaded one after the other with a ratchet click. Soldiers in black combat fatigues rose in a circle around the two men, rifles pointed at them. One stepped forwards.

"Hello, boys."

*

Agent Brennan led Hildy, Luca and Ryan to a waiting 4 x 4. "Guys, your country is in your debt. I wish I could tell you more about the project we're working on here, but – "

"We know," laughed all three friends together. "It's classified!"

Brennan saw them into the 4 x 4 before climbing into the front himself.

"You know the worst thing about this?" grumbled Ryan as the vehicle pulled away.

"Apart from being chased across the moors and almost shot at by a couple of nutters?"

"We won't be able to tell a soul!"

"There's worse than that," said Hildy, snuggling down into the comfortable seat, fatigue taking over. She smiled. "How do I explain to Dad what happened to his tablet?"

THE END